MW00875267

The **Sophia Day**® Creative Team-
Megan Johnson, Stephanie Strouse,
Kayla Pearson, Timothy Zowada, Carol Sauder, Mel Sauder

**A SPECIAL THANK YOU** to our team of reviewers who graciously give
us feedback, edits and help assure that our products remain accurate,
applicable and genuinely diverse.

© 2019 MVP Kids Media, LLC, all rights reserved

No part of this publication may be reproduced in whole or in part by
any mechanical, photographic or electronic process, or in the form of
any audio or video recording nor may it be stored in a retrieval system
or transmitted in any form or by any means now known or hereafter
invented or otherwise copied for public or private use without the written
permission of MVP Kids Media, LLC.

For more information regarding permission, visit our website at
www.MVPKids.com or send an email to info@realMVPkids.com
for any special requests.

Published and Distributed by MVP Kids Media, LLC
Mesa, Arizona, USA
Printed by RR Donnelley Asia Printing Solutions, Ltd
Dongguan City, Guangdong Province, China
DOM Feb 2019, Job # 02-006-01

Feeling **Arrogant &**
Learning **Humility**™

REAL
**mvp**kids®

# Olivia Uproots
## the Arrogant
## Weed™

SOPHIA DAY®

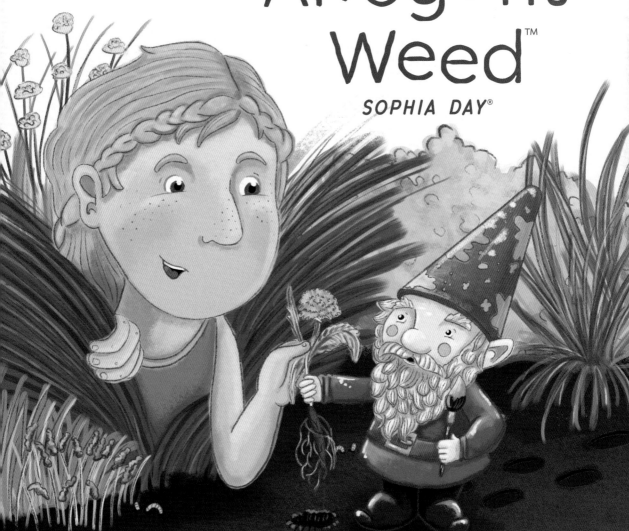

Written by Megan Johnson   Illustrated by Stephanie Strouse

Olivia and her sisters, Darcy and Marie, were enjoying their favorite hobbies. Olivia was working on another *award-winning* picture for the school art show.

"LUCY!" Olivia yelled to their oldest sister. "Marie keeps distracting me!"

Lucy stepped in to check out the problem.

*"Olivia, she's not even near your picture."*

"She's distracting me. Make her move," Olivia demanded.

"Your work isn't more important than hers," said Lucy.

"How about we do something else. Let's play a game."

"Okay, I'll get Draw-It!"

Olivia jumped up to get her favorite game.

"You always win that one. Let's find one everybody likes," Lucy suggested.

"You're just *sore losers*," said Olivia.

"Everyone needs an equal chance," said Lucy.

Olivia was happy when a phone call pulled Lucy away. Lucy always sided with her other sisters. "It isn't my fault I always win," she thought.

Lucy came back to let them know that Oma* had called. She was inviting the girls to help her in the garden.

All three girls jumped up to go.

*Oma is German for Grandma.

Olivia was first on her bike and sped down the street, while Darcy helped Marie with her helmet.

Olivia got to Oma and Opa's house in record time.

"Are your sisters coming too?" asked Oma in surprise.

"They're are on their way, but I wanted to pick my job *first*," replied Olivia.

"Your garden looks great, Oma!" Olivia exclaimed.

"I just do the planting. It's the gnomes who do the hard work to keep them beautiful." Oma winked.

Olivia loved Oma's garden gnome collection. When she was younger, she had made up names and stories for each one.

"What's *that?!*" Olivia pointed to a large box that Opa was carrying.

"That's our new raised garden bed. Liam and his dad built it for us. Isn't it nice?"

Olivia felt a wave of jealousy that someone else had created something beautiful for *HER* grandparents.

"Hi Liam. So you made that box?"

"I did the sanding and the staining. Dad used the power tools," Liam said modestly.

"You did a beautiful job. That's really something to be proud of," Oma said.

"Thank you," replied Liam.

Olivia was annoyed. "It's **just** a box. What's the big deal?" she sighed to herself.

Now her sisters had arrived and she wouldn't get first pick at what to plant.

Oma began directing everyone. "I'll be weeding. Darcy and Marie, you plant the flowers by the house. Olivia, you and Liam can plant the vegetables in the raised bed."

"I want it done right," Olivia declared. "I'll be just fine on my own."

As Olivia walked away to get the seedlings, she stumbled over the hose and tripped...

# Straight into the arms of a garden gnome!

"What happened? How did I..." Olivia began.

"Glad I caught you," said the gnome. "I'm Henric."

"Henric? *Henric!* The one who keeps the colors bright! How are you so real?" Olivia said in amazement.

"I'm as real as the stories you and Oma told," he replied. "Hurry, we need you underground."

Henric led Olivia to a
stepping stone. With a secret knock
and a short wait, the stone lifted.
Olivia followed Henric into the
## hidden world below.

There were tunnels in all directions.
Glowworms hung like string lights all around.
Gnomes scurried frantically.

Wildflower Garden

Vegetable Garden

Corner Garden

"Quickly, this way," Henric directed her.

"Why is everyone in such a hurry?" Olivia asked.

"It's a weed takeover!" Henric warned.

"We don't have long before it will be too late."

Henric led Olivia down a tunnel and explained, "Underground, there's a delicate balance. Flower roots **respect each other** and **share nutrients** in the soil. They give each other room to grow."

"Weeds start small, but they soon **become jealous** of the flowers, and think, 'I can be **taller**' or 'I can be **prettier**.'

They panic that there won't be enough space, so they wind around other roots to keep them from growing."

"Weeds are *terrible!* Now I see why Oma weeds nearly every day," Olivia said.

"You know, attitudes are a lot like roots. You can share your talents and lift others up, like a flower, or you can let confidence overgrow, like a weed, fighting to be the best and crowding out others," Henric explained.

"But what if I really *AM* the best at something?" Olivia objected.

"You can take pleasure in succeeding and doing well. However, pride turns into arrogance when you compare, compete or put others down."

Olivia brushed off his advice. She was here to be *a hero*, not to reflect on her pride.

"That's interesting," she said to Henric, "but how can I get rid of these weeds?"

"A garden is the reflection of the gardener. Search out and uproot the arrogance in your own heart, then the garden can heal."

Henric wanted to help her see how her pride had turned to arrogance. "See this disrespectful root? It tramples over others to gain all the good for itself. But respect sees the needs of others as important, too."

Olivia thought about the game they didn't play that morning.

"I'm like that root. I choose games and activities that I know I can win. Everyone would have more fun if we all had an equal chance. *I guess I don't have to win every time.*"

"Good! Now, see this little seedling? The weeds will choke it before it even has a chance to flower. Arrogance has no compassion for those who are weaker."

Olivia thought about Marie. It isn't easy to have a sibling with special needs. Olivia often felt like she needed to compete for attention. She sometimes used her sister's weaknesses to make herself feel stronger.

She stopped to wonder what it must feel
like to be Marie.

"I should be more helpful to Marie," Olivia said.
The weed *withered* at her touch.

"Yes," Henric agreed. "Use any advantage you have
to help others rather than putting them down."

"And what about that boy, Liam?" Henric prodded. What make you more worthy than he is to plant the garden?

"Well, it is MY grandma's garden. Why should he get to help?" Olivia defended herself.

"Oh, I see," the gnome said grimly. "You think that where you come from makes you more important than someone else? **That is** prejudice. Prejudice is judging someone's worth based on things they can't control."

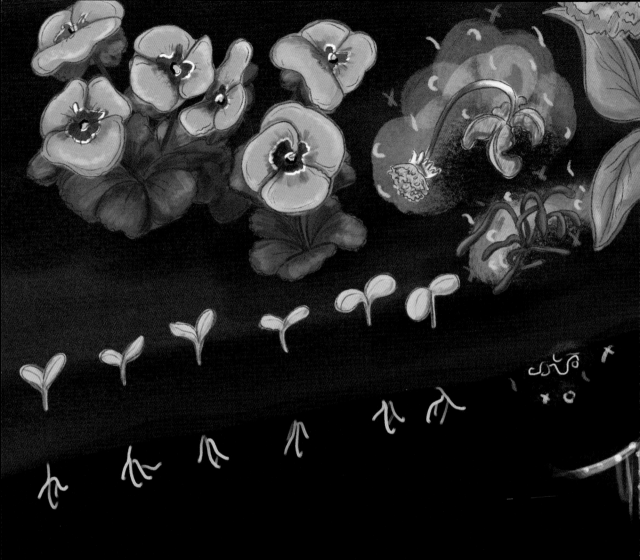

Olivia didn't consider herself to be prejudiced, and it did not feel good to realize that Henric was right. Oma always said that respect and compassion were more important than achievement.

Olivia answered, "Liam did really nice work on the garden bed. I should apologize for my attitude and congratulate him."

"Well, that ought to do it!" declared Henric.

Olivia looked around and saw all the roots of the weeds shriveling up.

"One last yank from above should heal the garden!"

Olivia climbed back up to the surface and uprooted the prideful dandelions.

She walked over to Liam.
"I'm sorry," Olivia apologized. "You built the beautiful garden box, and you ought to put in the first plant."

"What if I don't space them correctly?"
Liam questioned.

"Don't worry. You'll do a great job!
The gnomes secretly do the real work, anyway."

Olivia turned to her grandmother. "Oma, Liam
is doing a great job planting the vegetables.
May I finish weeding?"

"I'd appreciate that," her grandmother replied.
"But I thought you didn't like weeding."

"I'm learning not to always take the best things for myself. I might even enjoy it," Olivia said.

After some hard work, everyone said their goodbyes. Weeding had given Olivia time to consider how to **uproot** her arrogance.

She would need to change her attitude and her actions.

That night, Olivia helped Marie create her own masterpiece for the school's art show. She wanted to **share the spotlight** and help Marie shine, too!

You think that you're the best
At everything you do.
You don't consider others
When you only think of you.

Race to be the first;
Recount and tell your wins;
Make yourself the most important–
These are signs of arrogance.

Quick! Before the weed takes root,
Keep your pride in check.
This tiny self-important shoot
Can make your life a wreck!

Look deep in the tunnels
Of your heart and you will find
That putting others down
To get ahead leaves you behind.

Cut back judgment; clear out prejudice.
Sow compassion; plant respect.
Uproot all your arrogance.
Let humility take effect.

Be content to share the spotlight
Because by now you know
Tending to the needs of others
Will also help YOU grow!

# LEARN  & DISCUSS

Olivia wants to talk about how she learned to weed out arrogance. She started to understand how to handle her feelings of pride, and she wants you to learn too!

Being confident helps you make friends, try new things, find your interests and do your best when you face a challenge. Confidence says, *"I can do this!"* But arrogance is when your attitude about yourself begins to isolate you from friends, makes you try foolish things or keeps you from trying things that might be embarrassing. Arrogance says, *"I'll prove I can do this better than others!"*

*How do you explain the difference between confidence and arrogance?*

*Can you think of an example of when too much confidence might lead to arrogance?*

*Is it possible to pretend to be arrogant when you lack confidence?*

I used to think about myself most of the time. I focused on my projects, and got annoyed when someone distracted or interrupted me. I chose only the games I wanted to play, and always tried to get first choice. I felt like I was more important than others. That's arrogance.

*In daily choices, such as, which slice of pizza to eat or which television show to watch, are you thinking only of yourself or do you consider other's needs and wishes, too?*

*In what other situations is it important to think about others?*

*How does it feel when you put others first?*

I became upset when I found out that Liam helped build the flower bed. I was used to being the superstar and didn't like it when others got attention for doing great things. One way to know whether you're feeling and acting arrogantly is when you are unable to praise others for doing things well. A confident person congratulates others for a job well done, but an arrogant person feels threatened when others succeed.

*Have you ever felt threatened when someone else was praised for their good work?*

*What could you say or do differently to show confidence and care rather than arrogance?*

Henric explained that prejudice is when someone judges another's worth based on something they cannot control, like I believed that I had more right to plant than Liam did because Oma is my grandma. In reality, both Liam and I were invited to help plant and had the same right to do the job.

*Think hard about your attitudes toward others. Do you judge the worth of others based on their family, culture, skin color, height, abilities or other things they don't fully control?*

*Do you show preference to people who are beautiful, smart, wealthy, well-dressed or who look more like you?*

*How can you reach out to show kindness to someone whom you may have treated with prejudice?*

An arrogant person takes all the credit for a job well done. The opposite of arrogance is humility, or modesty, which means your self-esteem is not dependent on others' praise. A humble person does not *need* attention, expresses thankfulness and shares credit when others help them succeed.

*Which characters in the story were humble?*

*What did they say or do that displayed modesty?*

*Would you rather be friends with a humble person or an arrogant one?*

*What is one thing you can say or do in your life to act humbly?*

# How can you help your child balance confidence with humility?

**Help children know their intrinsic value.** Children who believe their accomplishments give them value are more prone to have either a deflated or inflated sense of self. When they know they are valued simply because they are your child/student, and not for what they accomplish, they will better balance confidence and humility. Children need to know they are loved and valued just for who they are.

**Help children set and achieve goals.** To learn humility, a child must first accomplish something. When children have set and accomplished a goal, help them identify feeling pleasure in the accomplishment rather than pride.

**Give specific, balanced praise.** Research is clear that too much praise serves to de-motivate a child rather than to encourage. When children are over-praised they may either doubt all praise and therefore not accept that they are good at anything, or put too much pride into the praise and become arrogant. It is important to give praise when a child meets a challenge with a great attitude or accomplishes something that took skill or dedication. Praise should be worded as, "You worked very hard to do well on that test" rather than "you're so smart." Unspecific praise and universal "everybody wins a trophy" rewards are usually counter-productive.

**Rehearse a response.** Teach your child that praise requires a response. To shrug off someone's praise is just as rude as basking in the spotlight. Rehearse appropriate responses that always include a "thank you." For example, when a child is praised for an art project it may be appropriate to say, "Thank you. My art teacher helped me get the background just right," or "Thank you. My grandma is a great artist and she teaches me a lot."

**Teach children to apologize.** Another mark of humility is the ability to apologize. Everyone must acknowledge that they are sometimes wrong. Help children to see when they have wronged others and guide them through a sincere apology. Modeling this yourself is the most powerful way to teach.

**Provide opportunities for children to serve others.** Teach children that all people are worthy of love. Give them valuable daily chores that serve the family, bake cookies for a neighbor, or let them clear out closets to donate toys and clothes. Serve the poor by keeping basic supplies in your car to give to people in need. Check with your local schools, churches, religious organizations, scout troops and non-profit organizations to find more ways to serve with your children.

**Help children show gratitude.** Showing appreciation for another's service will help combat feelings of entitlement while nurturing gratitude. Allow your child to stay a few minutes after school to help a teacher clean the classroom. If you have anyone providing services in your home, such as cleaning, yard service or home-based therapy, your child can prepare a baked treat, card or artwork to share. At home, create a culture of gratitude for each other and the roles each family member plays in keeping the household functioning.

*For additional tip and reference information, visit **www.mvpkids.com**.*

Meet the

# mvpkids®

featured in

## Olivia Uproots the Arrogant Weed™

OLIVIA WAGNER

Can you also find these MVP Kids®?

LIAM JOHNSON          AANYA PATEL

# Also featuring...

**LUCY WAGNER TORRES**
Sister

**DARCY WAGNER**
Sister

**MARIE WAGNER**
Sister

**GEORGE WAGNER**
"Opa"
Grandfather

**LIESL WAGNER**
"Oma"
Grandmother

**HENRIC**
*Keeps the
colors bright*

**BUTTER**
*Leader of
the garden*

**PINKY**
*Seed
planter*

**SCOOP**
*Digs the
tunnels*

**AQUA**
*Waters
the roots*

# Grow up with our **mvp**kids®

**CELEBRATE!™**
Board Books
**Ages 0-6**

Our **CELEBRATE™** board books for toddlers and preschoolers focus on social, emotional, educational and physical needs. Helpful Teaching Tips are included in each book to equip parents to guide their children deeper into the subject of the book.

help **me**™
BECOME
**Early Elementary**
**Ages 4-10**

Our **Help Me Become™** series for early elementary readers tells three short stories of our MVP Kids® inspiring character growth. The stories each conclude with a discussion guide to help the child process the story and apply the concepts.

## Don't miss out on our 3-part **STAND** anti-bullying series!

help me UNDERSTAND™
Elementary
Ages 6-12

Lucas Tames the Anger Dragon
SOPHIA DAY

Our *Help Me Understand™* series for elementary readers shares the stories of our MVP Kids® learning to understand and manage a specific emotion. Readers will gain tools to take responsibility for their own emotions and develop healthy relationships.

Help your children grow in understanding all kinds of emotions by collecting the entire **Help Me Understand™** series!

Miriam Lassoes the Worry Whirlwind
SOPHIA DAY

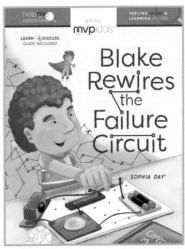

Blake Rewires the Failure Circuit
SOPHIA DAY

Sarah Sizes Up the Insecure Ant
SOPHIA DAY

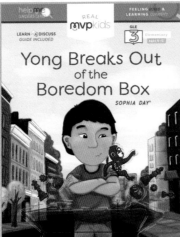

Yong Breaks Out of the Boredom Box
SOPHIA DAY

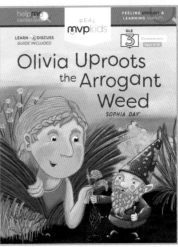

Olivia Uproots the Arrogant Weed
SOPHIA DAY

www.mvpkids.com